For Pat a

Tom and the Tinful of Trouble

by Nick Sharratt
and Stephen Tucker

SCHOLASTIC

With thanks to
David Fickling, Ness Wood
and John Peacock

Scholastic Children's Books
Euston House, 24 Eversholt Street
London NW1 1DB
a division of Scholastic Ltd
London ~ New York ~ Toronto ~ Sydney ~ Auckland
Mexico City ~ New Delhi ~ Hong Kong

First published in hardback in the UK by Scholastic Ltd, 1998
First published in paperback in the UK by Scholastic Ltd, 2000
First published in this edition in the UK by Scholastic Ltd, 2007

Text copyright © Nick Sharratt and Stephen Tucker, 1998
Illustrations copyright © Nick Sharratt, 1998

10 digit ISBN 0 439 94474 0

13 digit ISBN 978 0439 94474 8

Tom found the red paint.

It took him three seconds
to decide what to
do with it.

One.

Two.

Three.

It took him (*oof!*) three (*humpf!*) minutes to get the (*grrrrrrrrrrr!*) lid off the tin!

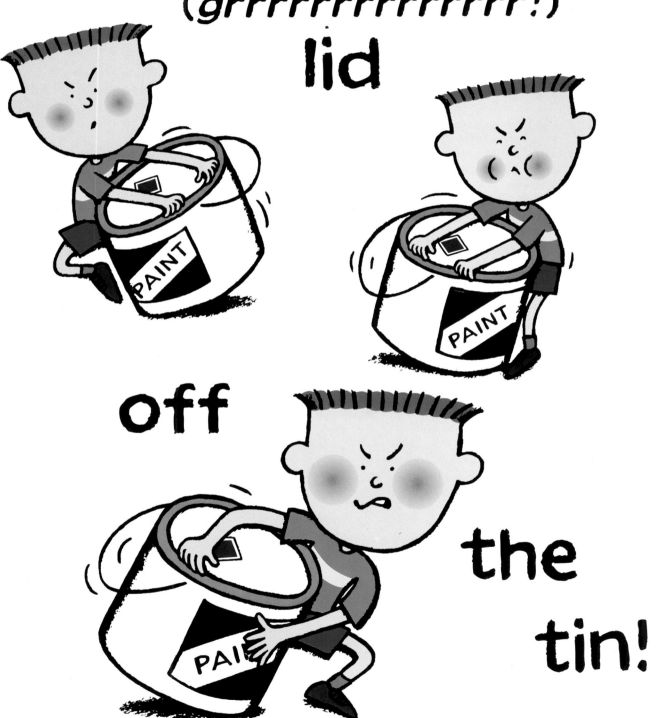

It took him three hours to paint the front room.

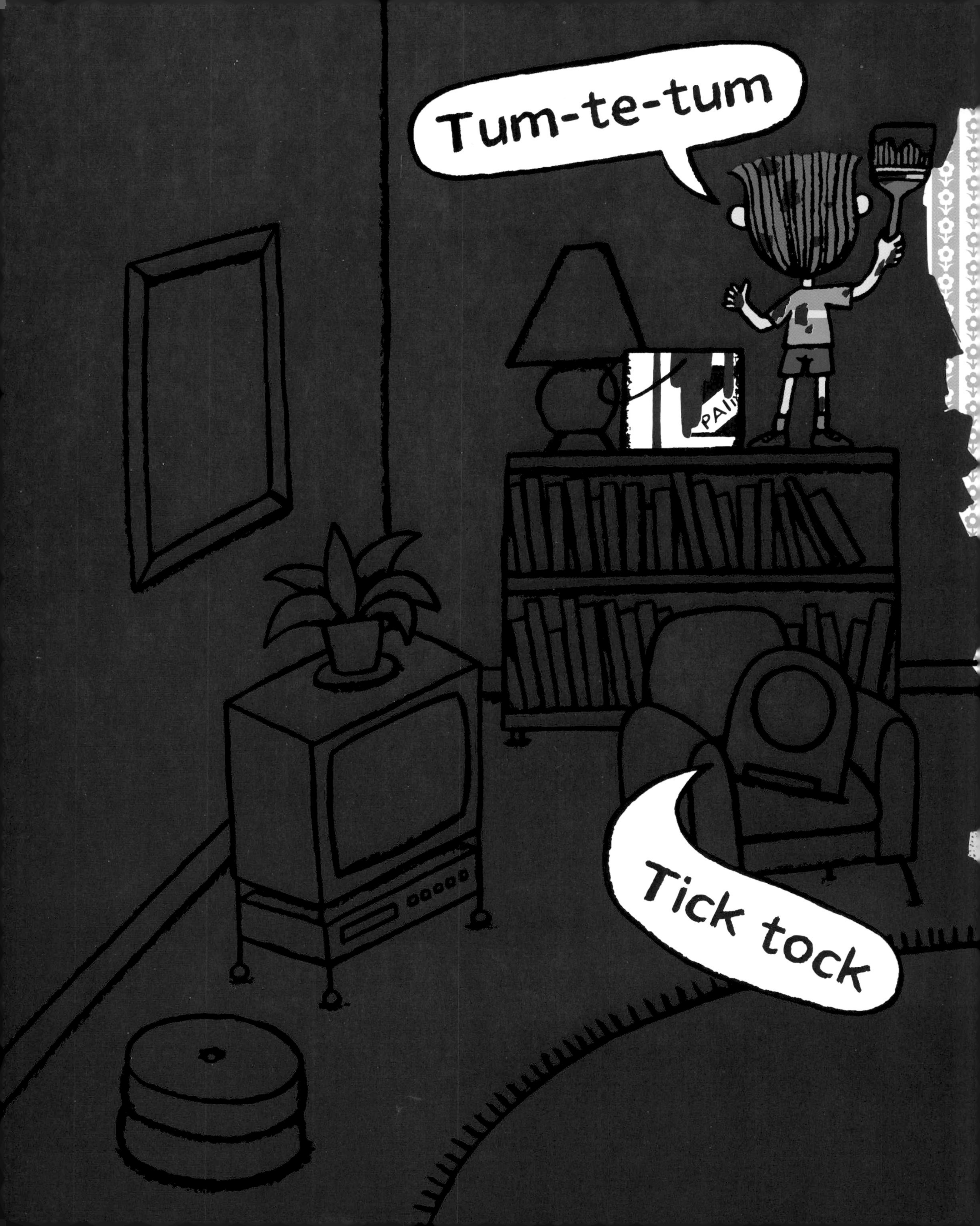
Tum-te-tum
Tick tock

Three hours.

Tick tock

Tom's mum came in.

It took her *ten*

nine

eight

seven

six

five

four

three

two

one

seconds to explode!

It took three weeks.

And this is how we did it.

 We had to get a skip

For the ruined bits of furniture.

 We stripped off all the wallpaper,

And went off to the store, Brrm

 To buy some tins of paint

(There were loads of different colours)

And pick a paper that we liked

 From all the ones we saw.

We sandpapered the woodwork

And we painted it with undercoat.

We started putting gloss paint

On the window frame  and door.

And that's when Mum decided

That she didn't like the colour,

So we stopped what we were doing

And we went back to the store.

Here's a list of what we painted:

The window and the skirting board

The bookcase  and the table

And the sideboard and the door.

 And this time Mum was happy

And I was even happier

Because I really didn't feel

 Like painting any more!

Mum hung the paper (by herself!)

Men came and laid the carpet

And after that we had to make

A last trip to the store . . .

For a sofa  and an armchair

 And a telly and a video

Some curtains for the window,

And a new rug
for the floor.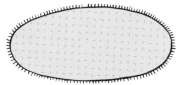

We also bought a little tree

(But that was for the garden)

And a footstool and a fruitbowl

And a nice plant in a pot,

Cushions,   lamps,   a mirror,

Some pictures of the countryside,

A clock,  a vase,

A photoframe,

And that's about the lot!

One year went by.

Two years

went by.

Three years went by.

Tom found the blue paint.